E
SEW , arc a
The cobbler's song

THE COBBLER'S SONG

THE COBBLER'S SONG

a fable adapted and illustrated by MARCIA SEWALL

A Unicorn Book · E. P. Dutton · New York

Library of Congress Cataloging in Publication Data

Sewall, Marcia.   The cobbler's song.
(A Unicorn book)
Summary: An unhappy rich man, disturbed by the
happy songs of a poor cobbler, resolves to make
the poor man as unhappy as he is.
[1. Folklore.   2. Shoemakers—Fiction]   I. Title.
PZ8.1.S4588Co   1982
398.2′1′0886853   [E]   82-9438
ISBN 0-525-44005-4   AACR2

Published in the United States by E. P. Dutton, Inc.,
2 Park Avenue, New York, N. Y. 10016

Published simultaneously in Canada by Clarke,
Irwin & Company Limited, Toronto and Vancouver

Editor: Emilie McLeod   Designer: Claire Counihan

Printed in Hong Kong by South China Printing Co.
First Edition

10   9   8   7   6   5   4   3   2   1

for Edgar, John and Douglas

Once upon a time a poor cobbler lived in the basement of a large house in Paris. He had to work from early morning until late at night to make enough money to keep himself and his wife and children. But he was happy in his dark little rooms, and he sang all day as he mended old shoes.

On the floor above him lived a very rich man. His rooms were large and sunny. He wore fine clothes and had plenty of good things to eat. Still, he was never happy.

All night long he lay awake thinking about his money—how to make more, or fearing lest it be stolen. Often the sun was shining in at his windows before he fell asleep.

Now, as soon as it grew light enough to see, the cobbler always got up and went about his work. And as he hammered, he sang. His songs floated up to the rooms of the rich man and woke him.

"This is just dreadful!" said the rich man. "I cannot sleep at night for thinking of my money, and I cannot sleep in the daytime because of the singing of that silly cobbler."

So the rich man sat down and thought the matter over.

"Hmm," he said to himself, "if the cobbler had something to worry about, he would not sing so much. I must think of a plan to stop him. Let me see, what worries men most?

"Why money, to be sure! Some men worry because they have so little. The cobbler has little enough, it's true, but that does not worry him. In fact, he is the happiest man I know.

"Other men worry because they have too much money, which is my trouble. I wonder if it would worry the cobbler if he had too much. That's the idea! Now I know what I shall do!"

A few minutes later, the rich man entered the cobbler's poor home.

"What can I do for you?" asked the cobbler, recognizing his neighbor but wondering why so fine a man should enter his little shop.

"Here, I have brought you a present," said the rich man, and he gave the poor man a purse.

The cobbler opened it and saw that it was full of shining gold pieces.

"I cannot take all this money!" cried he. "I have not earned it. Take it back."

"No," answered the rich man, "you have earned it by your songs. I give it to you because you are the happiest man I know."

Without waiting for any thanks, the rich man left the shop.

The cobbler turned the gold pieces out on his table and began to count them. He had counted to fifty-two, when he looked up and saw a man passing by the window. He quickly hid the gold. Then he went into the bedroom to count it where no one could see him.

He piled the coins up on the bed. How golden they were! How bright! He had never seen so much money before. He looked and looked at the money until everything in the room seemed golden and bright. Then he counted it slowly.

"One hundred pieces of gold! How rich I am! Where shall I hide it for safekeeping?"

First he hid the coins under the covers at the foot of the bed, which he could see from his workbench.

"The money makes quite a lump under the covers," he said. "Perhaps someone else will see it and steal it. I think I should hide it under the pillow."

While he was putting it under the pillow, his wife came into the room.

"What is the matter with the bed?" she asked.

The cobbler glared at her, and drove her from the room with angry words—the first cross words he had ever spoken to her.

Dinner came, but he could not eat a mouthful because he was afraid someone would steal his treasure while he was at the table! As he worked, not a note did he sing. By suppertime he felt worse. Not a kind word did he speak to his wife.

Day after day and night after night, the cobbler grew more and more unhappy, worrying about his money. He dared not go to sleep, lest he should wake to find that his gold had disappeared. He tossed and turned on his pillow.

But upstairs, the rich man was happy. "That was a fine idea," he said to himself drowsily. "Now I can sleep all day without being awakened by the cobbler's song."

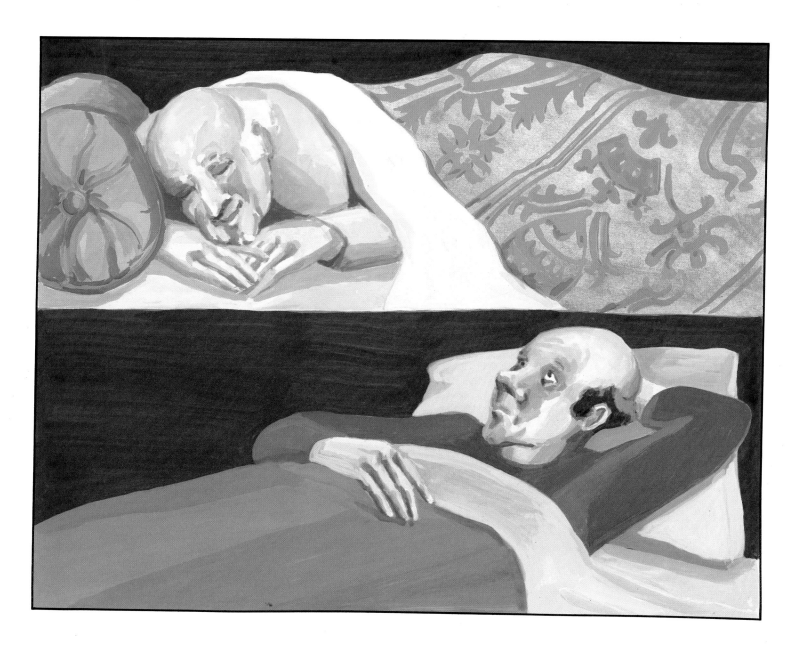

For a month, the cobbler worried over the hundred gold pieces. He grew thin and pale, and his wife and children were most unhappy. At last he could bear the worry no longer, so he called his wife and told her the whole story.

"Dear husband," she said, "take back the gold. All the gold in the world is not worth as much to me as your happiness and one of your glad songs."

How relieved the cobbler felt to hear her say this. He picked up the purse and ran upstairs to the rich man's home. Throwing the gold on the table, he smiled and said: "Here is your purse of gold. Take it back! I can live without your money, but I cannot live without my song."

Stockton Township Public Library

Stockton, Illinois